Contents

1	The Name Gan	1
2	Rescue Me!	5
3	Charming!	8
4	The Spell	14
5	Sisters	17
6	Fairy Tale Friend	21
7	Hip Hop	26
8	Class Act	30
9	Back to Reality	36
10	Dream Guy	40
11	Happy Ever After?	50
12	The Spell	54
13	LC Cool and the Quest for the Perfect Look	56
14	The Secret Life of LC Cool	62
15	The Big Night at the Ballroom!	64
16	Fairy Tale	72

Chapter 1

The Name Game!

The first problem is my name.

You won't believe what my mum called me. Well, maybe you will believe it. Maybe your mum is as crazy as mine.

My mum named me Elsie.

That's right. **Elsie**.

Try to see an 'Elsie' in your mind. What does she look like?

An old lady at a bus stop, right?

Maybe an auntie?

Or a gran?

This Elsie you see in your mind ... look at her feet. What does she have on?

Killer heels? No.

Comfy shoes? Yes.

Slippers? Maybe.

With zips.

Possibly tartan.

Go back to that Elsie you saw in your mind.

What is she wearing?

A cool jacket? No.

She's wearing a big old warm coat. Like some sort of horse blanket or bed cover.

Oh yes.

Cool?

No way!

And does she have a designer handbag over her arm?

No, she does not.

She has a shopping bag.

Maybe she even has a shopping trolley.

Possibly also tartan.

Here's my drawing of what a real Elsie looks like –

And this is me –

I am 15 years old.

I would love to be cool.

But my mum called me Elsie.

Yes, this is me, Elsie Cole.

4

Chapter 2

Rescue Me!

I was hiding in the school toilets. *Again.*

I could hear them just outside the door. They were after me. *Again.*

Meet my tormentors. The ones I'm hiding from.

First – their leader. The one, the only, Kitty Carter.

Pretty Kitty Carter. And her mates are with her, of course. I call them the Airheads.

Kitty and her Airheads all have the same look. It's the 'princess' look, like in all those celeb mags.

They're all slim.

They're all blonde.

I think Kitty's a natural blonde. *Maybe.*

They have long hair they can toss.

They have trendy shoes they can teeter in.

They have clear skin, which *always* has a light tan.

They have long eyelashes they can flutter.

And they have lips that are always moist and glossy.

They are princesses just waiting to be kissed.

They are living the fairy tale.

They've got it all.

And their mission in life is to make sure I know I haven't got anything.

I'm not pretty.

I'm not popular.

I'm not an 'It' girl.

I'm a 'What? Who?' sort of girl.

Kitty is pretty, pretty, pretty and like her name she is **catty**. She's always having a go at me. Every day she gets her claws in. Every day she pokes fun at me. I hate it. Which is why I was hiding in the toilets, waiting for Kitty and her mates to leave and go home so I could scuttle off to History.

If Pretty Kitty and the Airheads got me, it would be *me* who'd be History.

I heard the door slam. I heard the sound of their shoes clicking off down the hall. I heard the giggles and sniggers get fainter, more distant. I gave it another minute and then I made a mad dash for it out the door. I was out! I was off! I was safe!

I was ...

OOF!

What was that?

Chapter 3

Charming!

I was on the corridor floor in a heap. I had run into something.

In fact, I had run into *someone*.

It was a girl I'd never seen before. I'd knocked her down and she was lying on the floor in a heap too.

She made a much better-looking heap than I did.

She was slim. She had long legs and **great** shoes. She had coffee-coloured skin and shiny, shiny hair. She looked way too cool to be in this school. Even lying crumpled on the floor she looked cool.

I just looked crumpled.

And pink.

I blush all the time. But this time I really had something to blush about.

I realised she must be a new girl. This was my chance to introduce myself by saying something sparkling and witty, something seriously stunning.

"Um ..." I muttered, "ermmmm ... um sorry."

"Whew!" The girl picked herself up and brushed herself down. "You came out of there like a rocket!"

"Sorry ... sorry ... sorry," I muttered.

I was as red as a tomato now. A really red tomato. I was as red as a tomato that had gone to a fancy-dress party dressed as a post-box. Oh, I was **red** – and I was really, really, really sorry.

"No probs!" The girl smiled. "I was looking for someone to help me anyway. You just got the job!"

"Anything! I'll do anything," I replied. "What can I do?" At that point I would have licked her boots, I was so sorry.

"You can show me the way to History Catch Up," she said. "It's supposed to be in a room near here ..." The girl looked down the corridor. There were dozens of identical doors.

"Catch Up Class? That's exactly where I'm going!" I told her. That was true.

I led the way.

★★★

It was never that hard to find the Catch Up Class. You just followed the noise coming from Lee and the Losers.

Lee and his two loser mates were in my class and they did *all* the Catch Up lessons.

Just like me.

But while I at least *tried* to work, Lee and his band of losers focused on seeing how much fun they could have with poor old Miss Fisher.

At that moment their fun was making animal noises. Why? I didn't know. Probably *they* didn't even know. But Lee squawked and the Losers squawked too. Lee clucked. And the Losers clucked too. Then he made monkey noises, a bit of roaring and even the odd elephant trumpet.

I hadn't a clue what had set them off on this new line in fun but it was handy for me because I was able to slide into the class without being told off for being late.

I was late (and got told off) almost every day because I always had to avoid Kitty and her Airheads. That meant I had to sort of zig-zag to the class, ducking into corners and toilets on the way to escape from catty Kitty.

I nodded to the new girl to wait at the front of the room then I slumped to my desk and unpacked my bag, ready for another 35 thrilling minutes of extra work.

These classes were supposed to help us out if we'd got behind in a subject. I'd got behind in every subject in the world except Art so I ended up at Catch Up classes more or less every day. So did Lee and his Losers. They didn't care at all.

But I cared.

The new girl waited at the front of the class while Miss Fisher attempted to get Lee and his mates to do some work.

Watching Miss Fisher at work was like watching a tiny old lion tamer trying to control a pack of lions. A pack of lions that had eaten far too many sweets and washed them down with a couple of energy drinks. So it always took ages for Miss Fisher to get them under control.

At last Miss F took her eyes off Lee for a moment and turned round. She saw the new girl. "Oh!" she said. "I'd forgotten we would have someone new today." She opened a folder and asked for the new girl's name.

"Charmaine," said the girl. "Charmaine Prince."

Lee and his Losers began to wolf-whistle and howl and growl, but Charmaine kept her cool. She faced up to them and gave them a stare. It wasn't just cold – it was icy. She seemed to freeze them.

The whistling, howling, clucking and braying faded away, leaving the Losers clearing their throats and looking embarrassed. Miss F looked surprised and impressed. She smiled at Charmaine. "That's a good trick!"

Charmaine shrugged. "The trick is to stare into their eyes, and not to blink once," she said. "I read about it in a book once."

There was no doubt about it. Charmaine was **magic**.

She could charm anyone or anything. She'd put a spell on Lee for sure.

He was blushing like a little 6-year-old kid.

Chapter 4

The Spell

By the end of the class I had done more than half a page of my History homework. This was a bit of a miracle for me because I don't know much about History. Plus I can't spell well and doing anything with the noise of Lee and the Losers in the background was almost impossible.

I managed to have quite a good chat with Charmaine too. She sat next to me.

It turned out she'd just moved to the area. She was from London. London! I bet our little town seemed a bit boring to her.

She had hardly done *any* of the same work we'd done in our school so she was in all the Catch Up Classes. She was quick at catching up, though. By the end of the lesson she was explaining things to me!

Her new house was just around the corner from mine so we walked home together.

I felt great. It was like having a new best friend. She was sharp as a tack and a real laugh. I had always wished I could be witty, but at school I was always too busy blushing and stammering. Charmaine had a way of making me feel relaxed, so I could laugh and joke with her. And she laughed *with* me, not *at* me, like Kitty and her friends.

I felt really good – until I caught a glimpse of us in the Pound Shop window. There she was, all tall and thin and cool. There I was, all round and short, with my messy hair sticking out like a brush.

She looked like a gazelle, loping elegantly down the road.

I looked like a guinea pig.

A guinea pig with hard-to-handle, fly-away hair.

Charmaine saw me glance at my reflection and try to smooth down my mad hair.

"I've got a great anti-frizz spray," she said. "It makes your hair all smooth and shiny." She tossed her shiny curls, as if she was in a telly ad. "Come round to my place tomorrow after Catch Up Class and we'll see what it does for your hair."

Ooh! A New Best Friend *and* a makeover. Life was good!

Chapter 5

Sisters

I was still feeling fantastic as I walked into school the next day. I kept a look-out for Charmaine, but I didn't spot her anywhere.

And then she was there, leaning against the door outside the school hall.

She was surrounded. Everybody knew about her now. She was new. She was cool. She had it all and now she had everyone wanting to be her friend.

I could wave goodbye to my almost NBF.

I could imagine my almost New Best Friend fading away.

Even Kitty and the Airheads were interested. Of course they tried to have a go at her. They laugh at my name and they tried the same trick on Charmaine Prince.

"Charming, I'm sure," Kitty sneered. Then she and her Airheads started singing, "Prince Charming! Prince Charming!"

"Prince Charming! That's you, that is!" Kitty sneered.

"Yeah?" smiled Charmaine. "So you must be the Ugly Sisters!"

Charmaine flashed her sparkling grin and everyone was instantly charmed.

They all turned away from Kitty and talked to Charmaine instead.

Kitty and the Airheads slunk away. Defeated.

I stood back, amazed. Charmaine was sorted. It looked like Kitty and the Airheads wouldn't try picking on her again. Lee and the Losers were treating her with something like respect. And Guy – Guy couldn't take his eyes off her.

Guy was the guy of my dreams. He was gorgeous. And, yes, his name really was Guy. I'd fancied him for ages.

I've watched my share of films. I read more than my share of celeb mags. I have drooled over pics of plenty of gorgeous stars. But I could still say there was no one I fancied more than Guy.

Everything about him was gorgeous, from his cool, spiky, gelled hair to his brilliant, flashing smile. And he was gorgeous on the inside too.

He had never made fun of me.

In fact, he had never spoken to me at all.

Actually, I don't think he'd ever even *seen* me.

Every time I sneaked a look at him, he'd be staring the other way.

Or gazing at the ceiling.

Or the floor.

Yep, he found the manky old school floor more interesting than me, Elsie Cole.

Now Charmaine didn't seem to be very interested in me either. She had given me a little wave when I first arrived, but then she was surrounded again and I lost sight of her.

Oh well. The best friend dream was nice while it lasted.

Chapter 6
Fairy Tale Friend

It was a bit of a surprise when Charmaine sat down next to me in the Catch Up Class at the end of the day. Mind you, I was the only other girl in the class and she wouldn't want to sit next to Lee or a Loser, would she?

It was French Catch Up that day. I've never had a clue about French. The only thing I know is that, in French, tables, chairs and curtains have sex.

Not with each other, obviously.

It makes no sense ...

Our job was to write about the items in a room in French. We had to put 'le', 'la' or 'les' in front of each item. If we got these right we would show that we knew the 'gender', or sex of each bit of furniture. Madness.

"I think the French must be sex-mad," I whispered to Charmaine.

She flashed me the most brilliant smile and told me I was really funny. In a good way.

I almost floated out of the class. Then I followed Charmaine down the road to her house where – if you remember – she had promised to turn my wiry brown curls into sleek and chic hair that I could toss in the air while I announced *"I'm worth it!"*

Charmaine spent ages putting a lot of her expensive products on my hair. When she had finished I peered at myself in her bedroom mirror.

It did look a lot better but it was still a bit like all my school reports said – *'Plenty of room for improvement.'*

I practised shaking my shiny hair and made an effort to hold my tummy in. It needs quite a lot of holding in.

I practised a twirl and a smile.

Did I look cool? Did I look glam? Did I look shiny and sophisticated? No.

I just looked a bit mad.

I saw Charmaine looking at me so I said the first thing I could think of to distract her. "You've got a really nice room."

She *did* have a nice room. It was full of posters and photos and shiny medals.

"I used to do dancing competitions," Charmaine explained. "Those are medals for tap and ballet and jazz dancing – but now I do hip hop and street dancing." She paused. "Well, I did do hip hop, you know ... but that was where I used to live."

She showed me a video on her phone. It showed her spinning and kicking and leaping.

She looked great. And very, very happy.

"One of my mates at my old school filmed this," she said. "We had a great crew of dancers there. I miss them ..."

She looked really sad. I think I even saw a tear in her eye.

I hadn't realised that someone as pretty and cool as Charmaine could get sad and lonely too. I hadn't really thought about what it was like to be her.

It must be hard to be in a new town. A new house. A new school. She looked as if she had it all – but deep down she was just like me. A bit lonely.

"I've found a dance class near here," she said. "Tuesdays and Thursdays. 7pm in the Town Hall ... There's a Saturday morning class too ..." She hesitated. "I'd like to go along but I don't know anybody there ... Why don't you come with me?"

Well, what could I say? She'd just spent 20 minutes and loads of expensive stuff trying to sort out my hair.

I could hardly say, "No. Just go by yourself," could I?

"'Course I'll come!" I said.

But all the way home I kicked myself.

Why had I agreed to go to a dancing class? I had classes all day at school. I had Catch Up Classes after school. The last thing I needed was extra classes in the evenings and at weekends.

And *dancing*? Me?

Hip hop? Me?

I didn't hop and I was definitely not hip.

It was all going to be *terrible*.

Imagine me lumping about trying to dance!

Imagine the rest of the class all staring at me.

And laughing.

It was going to be a nightmare.

Chapter 7

Hip Hop

It was all I thought about the rest of the week in school. Should I tell Charmaine I'd changed my mind? Should I make some sort of lame excuse? Should I hide?

Should I leave the country?

Maybe I was making too much of it, but I couldn't get it out of my head. I hardly cared that I was in Catch Up On Everything class. I hardly cared about Kitty and her catty remarks. I hardly thought about Guy – well, not more than six or seven times an hour, anyway.

Thursday came around and so did Charmaine ... she came to my house to collect me.

She was wearing loose black cargo pants and a short grey-and-red top, and she had a scarf tied in her shiny curly hair. On her feet she wore some bright red baseball boots, which were half unlaced.

She looked **fab**.

I was wearing my old leggings and a jumper.

My hair was its usual brown bushy mess and I had on my old trainers.

I looked **fat**.

When we opened the door into the dance class I nearly died of embarrassment. Every face turned around to look at us. I could feel my face going from pink to red to scarlet. I was like a one-girl sunset.

The teacher was in the middle of scribbling on a big piece of paper pinned to the wall, but when she saw us she smiled and waved us in. Then she turned back to the paper and wrote '**Missy Masters**' in scrawly graffiti across it.

"You can call me Missy," she said. "Outside of here I'm just Miss Masters but we all have our hip hop names in the class."

Then she turned to Charmaine. "What's your name?" she asked. Charmaine told her. "I'll call you Charmy," said Missy. "That OK with you?"

"Cool!" said Charmaine.

Missy wrote 'Charmy' on the paper, then she reached for another colour of pen.

"And your name?" she asked me.

Oh, I hate my name.

I hate my look.

I hate myself.

But most of all I hate my name.

It is so uncool. It's not even slightly chilled. My name is just wet. You hear my name and you just think drip, drip, DRIP.

"Elsie Cole," I mumbled.

Missy reached for a neon pen and scrawled **LC Cool**, in big, bold graffiti right across the paper.

"Great name!" she said.

Everyone smiled and said, "Hi Charmy! Hi LC!"

All of a sudden, I felt cool.

I might **hate** the name Elsie but I **heart** the name LC!

"I'll always call you LC Cool from now on," Charmaine whispered to me. "This could be the start of a new you!"

Chapter 8

Class Act

My first dance class was better than I expected.

No. It was better than better.

It was *the best*.

It was brilliant.

It started with a warm-up – which means standing around and stretching. And then lying down and stretching.

I can do that.

Sometimes I can spend a whole weekend lying around and stretching. In bed!

Then we did some exercises to get started.

I'm not all that big on exercise.

I'm just big.

I tend to avoid PE. I find if you stand at the back of the line, shuffle back and don't make much noise, you can avoid most of PE. I've avoided it for years.

And sports! I just don't go there. It's easy – no one picks me for teams so I just mess about with the other no-hopers.

But here in this dance class, it was different.

Here I wasn't a no-hoper.

I was a hip-hopper.

I was LC Cool.

There were all sorts of people in the group and they weren't a bit interested in laughing at me. They were just interested in dancing.

And Missy and the group were really friendly and welcoming.

"Relax," she said to me. "There's nothing to it!"

Missy likes to sing out what she wanted us to do –

> *If you can move your feet*
> *and count to eight*
> *you'll be fine*
> *you'll be GREAT!*

And –

> *If you can move BOTH feet*
> *and count sixteen*
> *you'll have really*
> *made the scene!*

She was always singing and rapping.

The music was great and I felt great too.

"Just take it at your own pace," Missy told us. "Do what you can, and bit by bit you'll get it! Just have fun with it!"

"Just *pretend* you're good at it," she advised me. "Confidence makes it work. You can cover up a *lot* with attitude."

She showed me how to stand, how to look.

"*Attitude!*" she said. "You've got to *look* confident – and then you will be!"

We turned and we stretched and we stepped and we hopped and I got very red and sweaty but so did everyone else and not one person laughed at me.

There was a great feeling in that class.

When we took a break, I met the rest of the group. There was Yo Yo (real name Yolanda), Ali (real name Alison), Jay Jay and JoJo, and Billy and Turbo and Bo. (I have no idea what their real names were).

Here we were, all new to dancing, and Missy showed us everything bit by bit. She repeated it often and she smiled and she told us we were good. In fact, she said we were great. She said we were **brilliant**.

We were **stars**.

"1, 2, 3 and turn!" she said. "3, 4, 5 and step!" And 1, 2, 3 and hop."

"This is my style," she told us, "but it's not the only style. Play with the dance. Find your own style ..."

I think that class was one of the best things I've ever done. Oh, don't get me wrong. I wasn't a great dancer – yet. But I felt good. I felt full of life and I felt I *could* become a dancer. Anything was possible.

★★★

The next day when I woke up I didn't feel so great.

In fact, I felt terrible.

I was soooooooooooo stiff.

Every muscle in my body hurt.

Every step I took was an effort.

Today it wasn't '1, 2, 3, hop!'

It was 'step, step, step, ouch!'

'Step, ooh! Step Aaaaaaaaaaagh!'

I *limped* to school. I kept stopping to hold my back and rub my knees like one of those old ladies you see at bus stops. "You're not used to exercise," Charmy explained. "The more you do it, the easier it'll get."

I believed her. I believed anything was possible. You know how they talk about those horrible hairy caterpillars that grow up and turn into butterflies? I thought *that's me, that is. I'm ready to transform. I can do whatever I want. Everything is going to change.*

Chapter 9

Back to Reality

Well, maybe not *everything* was going to change.

Back at school, Charmaine went off to Maths. I was on my own, and Kitty and the Airheads saw their chance. There was no way I could run away from them. I was too stiff to run. I would have to stand my ground.

They really got stuck into me.

"I always said you were lame," Kitty smirked, "but you look *really* lame today!"

The Airheads giggled. Kitty was on a roll.

She had a go at my hair.

She had a go at my weight.

She had a go at my shoes.

Normally I would have run off and Kitty would have won. This time I had to stand and take it. So I took Missy's advice from the class and I stood there with attitude.

With confidence.

Kitty knew she wasn't getting to me as much as usual so she tried getting louder. And louder.

In the end, she was shouting. She went red in the face. She looked like a toddler having a tantrum.

It was odd, but her teasing and mocking just seemed ... childish. She would give me her best shot, her worst insult and I'd just find myself smiling like you would at a silly child.

Normally she can get me with "Oh poor little Elsie is blushing ... Is that a tear? Oh boo hoo hoo! Poor Elsie is crying ..."

But today I didn't feel like crying. I didn't even blush! Once I even laughed at one of Kitty's catty remarks.

Kitty's mouth fell open.

I felt amazing. I'd won.

So things were picking up for me – except in one area.

Guy.

He was still gorgeous.

He was still the guy of my dreams.

He was still as far away from noticing me as ever ...

I told Charmy all about it.

She gazed off into the distance as if she was far away in a dream.

"I may have the answer," she murmured. "Maybe I can make your dreams come true ..."

"Huh!" I said. "You'd need a magic wand!"

"It's my birthday, soon," Charmy said. "My mum says I can have a party and I'll invite you – of course. And I'll invite Guy and some of his mates too. And before the party I'll give you a makeover. What do you say to that?"

I said –

"THANK YOU! Thank you thank you ..."

Chapter 10
Dream Guy

To LC Cool

YOU ARE INVITED TO

CHARMAINE'S
BIRTHDAY PARTY!

SATURDAY AT 7PM

love from Charmy xxx

RSVP 477 6214

So – fast forward! A week had passed. I'd done more hip hop sessions. I was feeling great and it was PARTY TIME!

I was round at Charmy's working on my look. I had my clothes with me, plus shoes and some things to put in my hair.

Charmaine and her mum unpacked my bag of bits and looked at them.

"This doesn't look like your style," Charmy said.

"Exactly!" I said. "It's *better* than my style. It's the sort of thing Kitty would wear."

"Hmmm," said Charmaine's mum.

I was starting to think Charmaine's mum was a bit of a stick-in-the-mud. "Will you be able to dance in these shoes?" she asked, as she peered at my shiny, super-high killer heels. "Will you even be able to *walk* in them?"

"I don't care if I have to sit on rock like a mermaid," I said. "These are what ALL the celebs wear on the red carpet. They cost me weeks of pocket money. Tonight I'm going for glam," I told them. "Gotta get my Guy no matter what it takes!"

I was feeling ready for anything.

Charmaine's mum swept my hair to one side and pinned it up. Not bad.

Charmy stuck in a shiny hair clip at the side and gave it a twist. Better.

The magic make-over began.

First my bottom had to squeeze into magic 'suck-it-all-in' tights and then into a tiny skirt.

Charmy wasn't sure.

Charmaine's mum was not sure at all, but I knew what I wanted.

I wanted to be more 'Kitty' than Kitty.

Then my feet had to squeeze into the killer shoes.

The tan had to be sprayed on.

Then there was shadow and blush, and bronzer and gloss and more gloss.

And then I practised my witty banter to use on Guy.

Charmy and I had a plan all worked out. I was going to carry in a plate of snacks. I would take the snacks over to Guy and then I would devastate him with my witty banter, my charming smile, and my bang-on-trend shoes.

I would flutter my eyelashes and ... Well you'll have to imagine the rest. But it was going to be sooooooo great.

It was going to be MAGIC!

Charmy's mum wandered off to make the pizzas and snacks. After that, she promised she would stay upstairs and out of the way for the party itself. Charmy had wanted her to go out. In fact Charmy **begged** her to go out, but her mum said no.

Charmy's mum wasn't much fun, really.

After Mrs Prince had finally gone off to the kitchen I brought out the final touch ...

False eye-lashes!

Two pairs.

Extra thick.

My plan was to wear them both so I could have extra-long, extra-lush lashes, as seen on all the glossy pages of my favourite mags.

I had a page I ripped out from one of them –
it explained it all. We followed the instructions
and

... after a long time ...

... they were on.

It was a bit of a struggle and I seemed to
have glue more or less everywhere. And *wow*,
they were heavy. And *ooh*, they flapped when I
blinked.

I felt like I had some leggy spiders or hairy
caterpillars glued on my eyes, or maybe some
small mice. My eyelids felt heavy and I couldn't
make up my mind whether I looked gorgeous and
glam ... or sleepy and bored.

Plus, every step I took in my new shoes was
agony.

And I could hardly *breathe* in my outfit.

But no price was too high to get my Guy!

I couldn't moan, anyway – I had on so much
lip gloss I could hardly speak. My lips kept
sticking together. Gloss can really build up after
six or seven coats, you know!

Soon, the guests arrived. Guy was one of the first.

Guy!!!! My guy.

He sat on a chair near the window. There was no sign of his mates yet. And there was an empty seat next to him! Yes!

He looked a bit lost.

Charmy handed me a small tray of pizza bits, sausages, turkey twizzlers, nuts and crisps.

"You're on!" she said. "Over you go ... offer him one."

Off I went. I tried a sort of a cat-walk strut but it wasn't that easy. I had to hold the plate steady as I inched towards him and offered the plate. My feet were throbbing. My eyes were drooping under the weight of the lashes. I had to try hard not to groan as I sank into the chair beside him.

I had to be careful how I sat in the tight skirt, so I sort of *perched* and held myself steady as if I was about to start running in a race. I had to keep the plate level too. It was all so tricky that I hadn't said even a word to him so far. I gathered my courage and got ready for some witty banter.

There was a *long* pause.

"P-p-p-p-p-pizza bit?" I stammered, in the end. I offered the plate to him.

"Thanks!" he said, and flashed his smile.

I couldn't bear it. He was just so lovely. My mind went blank and I had to study my feet for a minute before I could even look at him again.

When I next looked up, he was staring at me. He looked like a rabbit caught in the head-lights.

"Um ..." he said.

"Um ..." I replied.

It was like a chat between two cavemen.

"Crisp?" I asked, after another pause.

He took one and I tried to summon up the courage to look at him but now he was staring at my shoes.

"I'm – " he started.

"A little sausage?" I broke in. "On a stick?"

He took one.

"What I'm trying to say," he said, "is that I'm – "

"Nuts?" I said.

"Right," his smile had gone now. "I get it."

I wanted to say that I hadn't meant that he was nuts. I wanted to explain I was just nervous. But I couldn't find the words. And what's more, my whole look was in melt-down. My eyes were stuck half shut. I could hardly breathe. I started to scramble to my feet but I stumbled on my stupid heels and dropped most of the snacks onto his lap. There were just a few bits left on the plate.

"Turkey Twizzler?" I cried and ran – well – limped away.

That's right. Those were my final words to the guy of my dreams. "Turkey Twizzler!"

I ran to Charmaine's room to grab my bag, rip off the lashes (ouch), kick off the shoes and pull on my coat. Then I was off, running down the road. I hoped I'd never see Guy again. I hoped I'd never see *anyone* again.

And who did I see?

Kitty and the Airheads.

It must have made Kitty's day. There I was, my feet bare and mascara all down my streaky, fake-tanned face. Who knows? I was probably muttering "Turkey Twizzler? Turkey Twizzler?" to myself like a mad woman.

Their laughter followed me all the way home.

Chapter 11

Happy Ever After?

Soon the texts started to arrive from Charmy.

Where R U?

Where R U?

WHERE R U???

Would you like to know where I was?

I was in my room at home.

I had a chair behind the door and my DO NOT DISTURB sign on the door handle.

I had the curtains closed and the light off.

I had the covers up to my chin and my face in the pillow and I was crying as quietly as I could. Which was not very quietly.

Floods of tears. Gulping sobs.

I was *never* going out again.

I was going to stay in my room for the rest of my days. I would never see Guy again. I would become a nun. I was a fool and a disaster and I wanted to leave town. No – I wanted to leave the country.

In fact, I'd have loved to leave the *planet*.

In the end I fell asleep.

When my phone woke me the next morning I just stared at it.

It was Charmy.

I didn't answer.

She didn't give up. Every two minutes the phone rang.

Ring Ring Ring.

In the end she came round to the house. We went down to the park at the end of the road for a chat. I told her all about it

Lots of times.

I do tend to repeat myself. Especially when I'm upset.

Each time I repeated a horrific detail I wailed a little less. In the end I was just making little moans and hiccups.

"It's not so bad," Charmaine told me. "Not really. It just *seems* terrible to you. No one else even noticed."

I began to feel a bit more calm.

"What did Guy do after I left?" I hiccuped.

Charmaine bit her lip. "Well ... he was pretty quiet and he had quite a bit of ... food on him so he had a go at rubbing it off with a damp tea towel. But that just smeared it a bit more and made him look as if he'd wet himself so ... then he went home. He'd gone before any of his mates got there. He didn't say much at all."

"Did he say anything about *me*?" I asked.

"No." She squeezed my arm. "Sorry. He really didn't say anything. He went away pretty fast."

"It's all over, isn't it?" I wailed. "It's hopeless. No 'happy ever after' for me."

"Try to forget about it," Charmy said. I could tell she wanted to change the subject. We had been talking about Guy for more than an hour. "We've got the weekend in front of us," she said. "It'll be ancient history by Monday and we've got our hip hop class in a couple of hours. That'll cheer you up!"

It was as if she'd turned into a cross between a cheer-leader and a mum. "Come on!" she said, as she pulled me to my feet. "The class will make you feel better – no one in the dance crew knows anything about the tragic Party Snack Disaster."

"It won't make me feel better," I moaned. "Nothing will ever make me feel better."

But I went.

And do you know what? By the end of the hip hop class I did feel bit better.

Chapter 12

The Spell

The truth is, it's really hard to think of anything else when you're twisting and turning, keeping in time and hipping and hopping and singing. (I can't help it. Sometimes I sing. I just love the music).

We learned some new moves. Some were new and some were what Missy called 'Old Skool'. And yes – you do spell 'school' like that in hip hop speak. With my spelling I'm pretty good at it!

That day we learnt the lock.

And we learnt the tick tock.

"Lock, lock, tick tock," I chanted to myself as I moved. The dancing worked its spell. Soon I felt a bit better – in fact, I felt good.

After the class, we all went to a cafe.

There I was, with a group of new, clever, funny friends in a cool cafe, having a laugh. We were making up raps about ourselves to go with the music we dance to. And then I glanced up and saw Kitty and the Airheads looking in the window. Kitty had her nose pressed up against the glass, peering in. She saw me in mid-laugh with Charmy and Jo Jo and Turbo. She looked surprised to see me having such a good time. In fact she looked a little disappointed. And jealous.

Chapter 13

LC Cool and the Quest for the Perfect Look

Over the next weeks I spent more and more time with Charmy and my new friends and less and less time worrying about Kitty and the Airheads. I just didn't have the time or energy to obsess over her.

I did still dream about Guy. Let's face it, some things – some boys – are just hard to get over. But I didn't spend my *entire* time thinking about him and the disaster with the party snacks.

The days seemed to go by faster. I chatted with Charmy for hours and I was kept busy with dance classes on Tuesday and Thursday nights and Saturday in the day. My dancing was getting to be really good! And I was hanging out with the hip hop crew in between classes.

The crew had a plan. *We were going to enter a talent contest.* Missy told us about it and she said we had the talent. We spent all our free time working up our act. Each of us was going to have a spot to introduce ourselves with a couple of lines of rap and then we were going to break into our hippest hip hop routine.

I worked hard at classes.

I practised in the morning before school.

I practised after school.

I practised at the weekends.

And if ever I had a few minutes spare – I practised some more.

I was getting good!

And I was losing weight.

I was slimming down. And toning up.

I was getting more exercise now than I'd had in my whole life.

And I was loving it!

My long evenings spent slumped in front of the telly with a family-sized bag of cheese and onion crisps were long gone. I felt so full of energy now, I didn't even find myself thinking about food. I just ate it, enjoyed it and moved on.

Who'd have guessed losing weight was so easy? I thought it was a science but now I know you just get off your bum, move about a bit and step away from the mega-packs of crisps and cola. I wasn't starving myself. I wasn't even thinking about getting fit – and the weight was just dropping off. Result!!

My leggings and jumper hung loose and baggy on me now.

I decided it was time for some new clothes.

We hit the shops. It was me and Charmaine in the Quest for the Perfect Look – On a Tiny Budget.

Actually Charmaine wasn't as helpful as I'd hoped she would be. She has great style so I thought she'd give great advice. I really wanted another makeover. But I wanted a better one this time!

"Shall I get this ... or that?" I asked Charmaine.

"Which do you think is best for *you?*" she asked.

Well, that wasn't very helpful!

I tried again. "Would *you* choose that – or this?"

"YOU choose," she told me. "Choose the look that suits YOU. Don't try to look like me, or like Kitty, or like anyone else. Find what suits *you*, LC."

Grrrrr! I was hoping for much more help. I wanted Charmy to *transform* me.

But it looked as if I was going to have to transform myself.

I decided to get clothes I could perform in. After all, I spent most of my waking hours dancing and we had the Big Talent Show coming up.

So I got some low-slung, loose cargo pants in very dark grey – or very light black depending on your point of view. I found an off-the-shoulder top in black with a grey and pink motif. I got a fab belt with stars on it and the best ever high-top sneakers in black with neon pink, yellow and grey squiggles. They were studded with tiny sequins and glass stars and they had neon pink laces that I planned to wear unlaced. They were a bit **too** big really but they were the only pair that colour left in the shop and I really WANTED them. My feet would need room to move anyway. And I could always wear thick socks. If I was desperate. Which I'm not.

I got loads of hair things and earrings and bangles and stuff too.

I looked **the bizz**.

LC Cool. That's me!

Chapter 14

The Secret Life of LC Cool

I couldn't wait for the Big Night.

The talent contest.

And I wasn't the only one thinking about it.

All round the school there were clutches of kids discussing it, planning for it, trying to get tickets – or practising their acts. It was the biggest thing to happen in our town since ... forever.

Kitty and her Airheads had got their tickets. Kitty waved them in my face and boasted. "It's in the Town Hall," she crowed. "In the ballroom!"

She hadn't a clue that I go there all the time for dance classes.

I have a secret life and LC Cool is my secret identity!

Kitty was planning on entering the contest. "With these looks, how can I lose?" she said.

She had decided to be the front singer of a group she'd made up and her Airheads were backing her. She would sing and strut and they would go "Oo Oo" behind her.

Only problem was – Kitty *can't sing*.

She sounded like a cat in pain.

One time I even saw one of the Airheads put her hands over her ears.

I tried to get near them to take a closer look but Kitty just about spat at me. "Get back to your corner, no-hoper!" she laughed.

Her Airheads joined in with the jeering but it just didn't get to me any more. I was LC Cool, hip hopper and I knew I was going to the Big Night. And I knew I was going to be great.

I couldn't wait.

Chapter 15

The Big Night at the Ballroom!

Oh, the days can crawl by when you're waiting for something to happen!

It was three weeks till the BIG NIGHT and it felt like three years. Or three hundred years.

Still, it gave us a chance to perfect our act.

It also gave me a chance to find out who was going to be at the big event. There was a list.

Kitty and the Airheads were on.

So were Lee and his Losers.

And so was Guy.

That's right – Guy was going to be there!

My heart gave a little flutter, like a teeny, tiny, trapped butterfly.

Or like trapped wind.

I was on the list too, of course, but my name was listed as LC Cool, so as far as anyone knew I wouldn't be there.

★★★

At long last, the big night arrived. Missy came to collect us in her funny van – it's bright orange like a pumpkin. "Your carriage awaits!" she smiled as she opened the door.

One-by-one we piled in. We all looked fab. I had my new clothes on. I'd tried them on a few times in front of my bedroom mirror but otherwise I'd saved them for tonight, so they were all crisp and new. Charmy and me and my bedroom mirror were all agreed. It was MY look and it was fabulous. Now it was time to try it out in public.

Charmy had added a few finishing touches. She'd tied my hair up in a funky way and added a pair of sunglasses.

I looked at my reflection. I hardly recognised myself.

I was *transformed*.

"You all look like stars," said Missy. "Now just enjoy yourselves and have fun out there!"

It was going to be a magical night.

A little bit later the nerves had kicked in and I wasn't so sure any more. I watched everybody arrive. Then I stood at the side of the stage and watched the other acts.

Most of them were a bit lame. Lee and the Losers did a comedy routine. Lee cracked up but the audience weren't so impressed. The judges were pretty hard on them too.

Kitty and the Airheads did their thing and the judges were even harder on them. The head judge was the worst. He was harsh. He addressed his remarks to Kitty.

"You can't just depend on looks," he said. "This is not a catwalk – it's a *talent* contest. The

66

only talent you showed was the ability to murder a wonderful song. It was painful to listen to. It sounded as if a cat was being strangled."

Once he'd hit on the cat thing he kept going for it. "It was a CATalogue of CATastrophes," he smirked. He looked so pleased with himself. "You just CATerwauled ..."

Kitty the bully had met a MUCH bigger bully.

She stomped off the stage.

Guy was on next. He and his mates had put together a rock band.

It wasn't bad, but it didn't *rock*.

Then a little kid turned up with a 'performing dog'. It was a cute dog but it wasn't the greatest performer.

Mainly it ran around and woofed. Most dogs can do *that*.

The next act was a juggler who dropped his balls.

"Oh! My balls!" he shouted. He didn't mean it to be funny but it was.

We were next.

I began to feel a bit faint and shaky. I had to keep whispering to myself, "You can do it! You can do it!"

"LC?" said Charmy. "We're on."

We stepped out into the spotlight.

We were in a different class from the start.

We had put in the work.

We were slick.

We were professional.

Missy had worked on the music and the lights and we were dressed to impress.

Plus we could actually dance.

One-by-one, we went on stage, struck our pose and did our rap intros:

Call me Missy
I ain't no sissy!

Call me Jo Jo
See me go go!

Charmy's my name
Dancing's my game!

One-by-one, all the crew gathered. I was last on stage.

I'm LC Cool and I'm no fool
Give me a chance and watch me dance!

Then we all shouted:

We're the Missy Crew
We know what to do!

The beat was banging, the lights were flashing and we STORMED it. Flips, tricks, moves, grooves – we did them all. Lock, tick tock, turn, twist. Step, hop hop, and stop.

The audience were on their feet in seconds. Even the judges were clapping along.

I could see Guy down there in the audience, watching. I could see Kitty and the Airheads, green with envy. Even Lee was paying attention, which for him is a miracle.

I was on top of the world.

It was a triumph!

We stopped and took a bow. The audience were cheering. I could see Kitty and the Airheads muttering, "Who is that girl?"

They *must* have known that it was me – but they couldn't believe it.

I could see Guy gazing at me with – well, it looked like admiration.

I just couldn't help it. I wanted to go that extra mile – I couldn't stop. I gave an extra spin, a huge leap and a high high HIGH kick.

My spirits soared.

So did my shoe.

Yes.

My bit-too-big,

not-laced-up,

black and neon-pink, sparkly baseball boot flew off and went shooting off into the audience.

The audience went "Ooooo!"

The audience went "Aaaa!"

I went "Noooooooooooo!"

Up and up it went.

The little starry glass studs caught the spotlight and twinkled like stars.

Then it twirled gracefully in the lights and down it fell

down

down

down

to land with a thump

smack –

– on Guy's upturned face.

Yes. He was literally floored by me.

Yes. I was literally a knock-out.

I turned and ran – well, hopped – off the stage and out of the stage door. One shoe on and one shoe lost, I lurched along like the Hunchback of Notre Dame until I found shelter in the nearest bus stop.

I sat there and sobbed. Once again I was a figure of fun.

In front of everyone.

In front of Guy.

I was a total failure.

Chapter 16
Fairy Tale

I huddled in the bus shelter, shivering and sobbing with my one damp, bare foot bleeding. I must have run over something sharp on my mad dash away from the ballroom. All my dreams lay in tatters around me.

My beautiful shoes were no more. I had blood and rain on my lovely clothes. My hair was falling down. I looked like a bundle of rags. A bundle of rags with one shoe on.

And that's when I heard footsteps approach

Oh no! I didn't want to meet anyone here.

Or anywhere, for that matter.

Ever again.

I heard a voice calling my name.

It sounded familiar.

Oh, no.

It was Guy. The last person I wanted to see. He came out of the rain, calling my name and looking around. He was carrying my shoe.

I tried to shrink into the shadows and I nearly managed, but just then a car swept by and its headlights lit up the bus stop. I was in the spotlight again.

Guy came right over. "I've been looking everywhere for you!" he said. "Look!" He showed me the shoe, and then he went down on his knees in front of me and wiped the worst of the rain and blood off my foot. He slipped the shoe on to my foot. I could hardly look at him. He got out a clean tissue and handed it to me. I blew my nose. I sounded like an elephant with a really bad cold but I was past caring.

"Go on," I said. "Laugh at me. Get it over with."

"Why would I want to laugh at you?" he said. "You were great. Everyone thinks so but you ran out before you could pick up your prize." He took a shiny medal out of his pocket. "Your crew got the prize for best act of the night."

"But my shoe!" I wailed.

"They loved it! The sparkly shoe flying through the air, missing the judges by inches and ending up in the audience. They thought it was part of the plan." He smiled and rubbed his nose. "It hurt a bit."

I realised that his nose was about twice its normal size.

And red.

In fact, it looked like he had a satsuma stuck on his face.

He winced when he saw me looking at him. "I know I look terrible," he said, "and I know you think I'm a joke but I ..."

"I don't think you're a joke!" I cried.

"Why do you play tricks on me then?" he asked. "Dropping food on me, saying I'm nuts, calling me ..." he gulped, "a Turkey Twizzler?"

"I never called you that!" I said. "I ... I ... I ... I think you're great. I think you're fantastic. I've always really liked – "

I stopped myself, sure I'd said too much. I thought he was going to turn and sneer at me.

But no.

Instead he said, "I've always liked you too – but you never speak to me. You hardly even looked at me at the party. You looked so bored, like you were half asleep. And you didn't even sit down with me. It was like you wanted to be ready to run away as soon as you got the chance. I was trying to ask you – " Now he was the one to stop.

"You were trying to ask me what?" I asked.

"I was trying to ask you if ... if ... you would ... go out with me ... sometime .. .if you're not too ..."

"YES!" I shouted, leaping to my feet. "**YESSSSS!!**"

I hope I didn't sound too keen.

"But I thought that you thought I was an idiot," he said.

"Well, I thought that you thought that I was an idiot," I told him.

"But I thought that you thought that I thought ..."

Yeah. We had lots of talking to do.

Lots of explaining.

But we had a date to look forward to and all the time in the world to explain ourselves to each other.

And then, who knows?

We might live happily ever after.

Or does that only happen in fairy tales?